This is to the boys...
Devin and Kai

Copyright © 1991 by Urban Research Press, Inc.
840 East 87th Street, Chicago, Illinois 60619
All rights reserved
Printed in Mexico
First Edition

Library of Congress Cataloging in Publication Data

Deloch-Hughes, Edye, 1959-
    I like gym shoe soup / by Edye Deloch-Hughes: illustrated
    by Darryl Hughes.
      p.   cm.
  ISBN 0-941484-11-4: $10.25
  1. Goats--Fiction. 2. Stories in rhyme.

I. Hughes, Darryl, ill. II. Title.
PZ8.3.D388Ial 1991
[E]---dc20   91-22328
                                            CIP
                                            AC

I LIKE GYM SHOE SOUP

by
Edye Deloch-Hughes

illustrated by
Darryl Hughes

I am a goat.
My name is Jimmy.

You may have had lunch.
I haven't had any.

But I have a taste
for a bowl of soup.
A bowl of gym shoe soup.

Don't you laugh.
My tastes are different.

You may like carrots
in your soup.
You may like chicken
in your soup.
You may like noodles
in your soup.

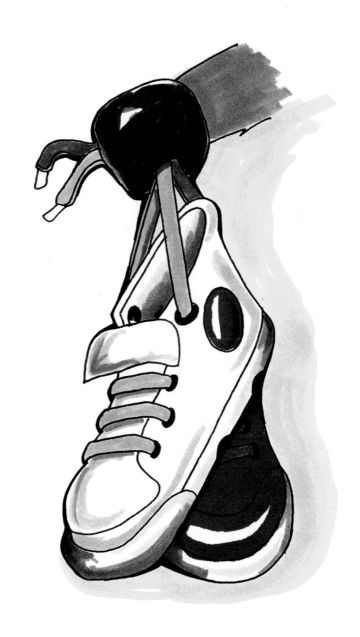

But I like gym shoes in my soup.
I like gym shoe soup.

I am a goat.
And goats eat grand.

If I made soup,
I'd add tin cans.

And fish bones
in my gym shoe soup.

And pennies
in my gym shoe soup.

And crabgrass
in my gym shoe soup.

Yes, I like gym shoe soup.

I'm almost home.
I smell my lunch.

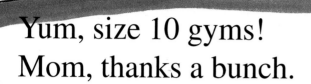

Yum, size 10 gyms!
Mom, thanks a bunch.

With shoe strings
in my gym shoe soup.

And worn soles
in my gym shoe soup.

And sweat socks
in my gym shoe soup.
Umm, I love gym shoe soup.

Oh! By the way...
Do you want to taste
my gym shoe soup?